Croc gets a snock

Mairi Mackinnon
Illustrated by Fred Blunt

Knock knock. "Who's there?"

"Hey, wake up, Croc!"

"I'm late! And there's so much to do –

I need new shoes, a new bag too.
I'm due at The Zoo at twenty to two."

Croc gulps her breakfast,

grabs her stuff.

She runs, but she's not quick enough.
"I've missed the bus!" She's out of puff.

Hic

Now Croc's in town. "It can't be true!"
The shoe store door says CLOSED TILL 2.

She sighs. "These boots will have to do."

It's party time! The Zoo looks fine.
The lions and rhinos wait in line.

The hippos hold a birthday sign.
But where is Croc?

"We'll have to wait. She's always late."

"At last! Come on, let's celebrate!"

Croc swallows quickly.
"What's up, Croc?"

"Unwrap your presents, Croc."
Croc picks a box...

...and gets a shock.
     "CUCKOO! CUCKOO!"

"My gosh! I almost dropped the box."

"You've never seen a cuckoo clock?"

"Hey, Croc! Guess what?
Your hiccups have stopped!"

"It was the shock."

"It's a tip-top tick-tock cuckoo clock!"

About phonics

Phonics is a method of teaching reading, used extensively in today's schools. At its heart is an emphasis on identifying the *sounds* of letters, or combinations of letters, that are then put together to make words. These sounds are known as phonemes.

Starting to read

Learning to read is an important milestone for any child. The process can begin well before children start to learn letters and put them together to read words. The sooner children can discover books and enjoy stories and language, the better they will be prepared for reading themselves, first with the help of an adult and then independently.

You can find out more about phonics on the Usborne Very First Reading website, **www.usborne.com/veryfirstreading** (US readers go to **www.veryfirstreading.com**). Click on the **Parents** tab at the top of the page, then scroll down and click on **About synthetic phonics**.

Phonemic awareness

An important early stage in pre-reading and early reading is developing phonemic awareness: that is, listening out for the sounds within words. Rhymes, rhyming stories and alliteration are excellent ways of encouraging phonemic awareness.

In this story, your child will soon identify the *o* sound, as in **Croc** and **clock** or in **stopped** or **what**. Look out, too, for rhymes such as **due – Zoo** and **fine – sign**.

Hearing your child read

If your child is reading a story to you, don't rush to correct mistakes, but be ready to prompt or guide if he or she is struggling. Above all, give plenty of praise and encouragement.

Edited by Jenny Tyler and Lesley Sims

Designed by Caroline Spatz

Reading consultants: Alison Kelly and Anne Washtell
University of Roehampton

First published in 2013 by Usborne Publishing Ltd., Usborne House, 83-85 Saffron Hill, London EC1N 8RT, England.
www.usborne.com Copyright © 2013 Usborne Publishing Ltd.